LITTLE BOOK

Unfulfilled Desires

Ro Desire

Dedication

This book is dedicated to every woman who has ever dared to be uninhibited

Acknowledgements

To all the women who read my writings and encouraged me to share it with others by writing a book, I want to thank you. If it weren't for your constant encouragement and words of affirmation when I felt I wasn't good enough, I would not have gone down the road of becoming an author. I owe it all to you!

Copyright

Table of Contents

"Quickies weren't her thing. For me...they were life fulfilling."

Pandora's Box

She walks behind me and ties a scarf around my eyes. It's dark. I can't see. I feel her soft skin brush against mine. We are naked. She walks me to the bed...lays me down. Her hands explore my body. I feel myself relaxing; anticipating what's going to happen next. Just as I'm beginning to trust her, I feel a second pair of hands on my thighs. The hands are delicate, soft. I speak, " what's going on?" A finger places itself upon my lips in the attempt to hush me. A pair of lips leaves a trail across my chest...stomach...inner thighs, tops of my feet, while a second pair of soft lips press themselves against mine. Two women...it must be. I feel the woman who's tracing kisses along my thighs and realize her hair is loc'd. Long. My lady's hair is loose natural. I gasp as Ms. Locs parts my thighs, and then licks my sweet spot. Caught off guard, I grab her hair. I arch my back as I kiss my lady and suck her tongue. She whispers in my ear, "that's right, just let go." She plays with my breast, while teasing my nipples as Ms. Locs massages my clit. I'm aroused in multiple places and the blood running through my veins has risen in temperature. My lady straddles my face. My mouth waters. She sits. I part my lips and invite her mound inside. I suck aggressively, the aggression matching my mood. While in between my thighs, Ms. Locs inserts her fingers. It's as though she's opening me up with the intentions to fuck me. She grinds her hips on my face as the other plays a game of passion in my honey well. I feel Ms. Locs stop. She then returns. I feel her part my legs with her knees. Then I feel something hard enter me. She's gentle, but the feeling is intense. I grip my arms around the thighs of her riding my face. I close my eyes tight as the other woman fills me up. Her hands grip my thighs. Her pelvis grinds against mine.

Moans escape my lips. I lick...suck...softly nibble...and massage the clit that's so swollen for me. The harder Ms. Locs fucks me, the harder I grip my lady's thighs. The wetter I get, the harder I suck her clit. It hurts. I like it. My body melts like butter as I put my nails in my lady's back while slipping my tongue deep inside her secret place. The hard strap goes deeper and I yelp...In pleasure. Ms. Locs is fucking me mercilessly and I'm taking every inch of her, hungrily. She stops. Slowly pulls out. My lady dismounts my face. I'm instructed to bend over...to get on all fours. Seconds pass and I feel a firm grip of my hair guiding my head down to her pussy. Ms. Locs is more hairy than I'm used to. Her smell is sweet. Clit swollen. She's a stranger whose offering me dinner and I willingly feast. I, myself, am so turned on so I lick, suck, and explore Ms. Locs as my lady reenters me from behind. I wrap my arms around thick thighs...thighs much thicker than my lady's. Skin smooth. I imagine she's Nubian. My lady enters me. She's less aggressive and fucks me slow. Each stroke, I mimic on the clit that's in my mouth. My lips are wrapped around her large swollen clit causing her to grab my hair. She moans...I moan...my lady moan...we are three women in sync. I can't see this woman who I am pleasing. I imagine her to look as yummy as she taste. Sweetness escapes her secret place. Her thighs clinch around my head. She screams. Low. I continue, allowing her to flow in my mouth. Her scream causes my lady to fuck me with rage. I suck her clit harder to mask my screams. She grips sheets...pillows...my hair. I'm...about...to...explode! As I climax I pull her strap out of me. I turn my body so that I can taste my lady while I'm floating on cloud 9. She climaxes. I needed her to flow in my mouth, too. Something about that drives me crazy. Still blind folded, we lay there catching our breath. There's six breasts rising and falling. I feel someone get up...she rubs my face...kisses my cheek...then closes the bedroom door behind her. I hear the front door open, then shut. My lady takes the blind fold off...stares me in my eyes...tells me "happy birthday." I smile. Blush. I'm shy. I tell her, "thank you" with my eyes. In this moment, all I can think about is this mystery woman who exited my life just as quickly as she entered it. I bite my lips. Pandora's box has the kitty-kat curious to explore...again.

"Temptation has my insides on fire. I want you. Period. Living selflessly has my body going without. A thirst that isn't being quenched has me desiring waters from a forbidden spring well. If only I was boundless..."

She Ain't It

It's dark. I imagine the woman laying in the dark is the woman who has stolen my heart. I kiss her body and caress her skin. As I lay in between HER thighs I hear YOU begging me to taste you…to please you. I kiss her. Lips the opposite of yours…everything the opposite of you. I proceed because I need to release tension. A stress has build up inside of me that scream to be released, temporarily. I close my eyes tight because I feel that will help aid in the attempt to forget about you; to forget the love we've made. Shutting you out has become unsuccessful. I'm running a race with each step that I take, the finish line moves further away. I taste her. She moans. A sound that does not make me squirm. I taste her. A taste that is foreign. My taste buds have become accustomed to you. She climaxes. It scares me. Her sounds are different from yours. It breaks my trance. For a second I was somewhere else...with you...just us two. I'm now laying on my back…my right nipple in her mouth. Naturally, my body reacts. She touches me. I'm not wet. She kisses me all over and teases my nipples…my hot spot. I'm getting wet. My body starts screaming. My body is betraying my mind. I still believe my body belongs to you. My clit is throbbing. Silent screams escape my lips as I grip the sheets in the attempt to regain my composure. I know this is not what I want. Casual sex. To cum casually doesn't hold the intensity of climaxing from the woman who holds my heart in her hand. Yet, I allow her to wrap her lips around my clit. She is putting in work. It's as if she's been waiting for this moment forever. I lie there...mad that my body won't listen to my heart. Upset that I have allowed myself to become so vulnerable. I whisper your name…loud enough to be heard, low enough to be mistaken for words of ecstasy. I'm single…a single woman whose heart is still taken.

Unavailable. I cum. I scream. I grip the sheets. I cry. Tears that scream out "I belong to someone else...only they don't belong to me!" The woman who I desperately need does not want me, unfortunately. Finally, my body calms down. My brain refocuses. I feel empty. I roll over in the fetal position. Tears fall till I fall...asleep.

"My breathing is in sync with the melody of your words..."

Stranger...Danger

Handcuffed. The undesirable, turned desirable position I found myself in with a complete stranger. Without prior conversation...lack of vocalized words of limitations...she took control of my body and permanently wrote her story over every square inch. Each sensual touch caused me to forget how to breathe. With every new feel she formulated, my heart raced, and lips parted to let out soundless pleads for mercy. She fucked me with a sexual vigor that made me question every intimate partner I had up until that point. Every desire was erased, every fantasy...recreated. My thirst was quenched in a way that provided substance to that sacred spot which lie deep within my womanhood. I was her new coitus endeavor, and like an addiction, she was my surreptitious cocanism.

"Gasping. The equivalent of what is happening between my thighs. Pulsating and welcoming a phantom touch. Inhaling and exhaling a thought that may never be. "Damn. I'm frantic over an imaginary lullaby."

Damn

Her expression said a lot. Exhausting, the only way to describe the night ahead. Simultaneously, she gripped my locs and brought my face to her pussy. My lips parted and allowed her large mound to enter. She gripped my locs tighter and I screeched. I knew that meant she wanted me to suck harder. I obliged. That wasn't enough. She yanked my head up and slapped me. My eyes closed tight as I bit my lips. Moments like these, when her hormones were raging outta control, she called me over to her place. I was her sex toy, which translated to "little bitch". Face still stinging, she began fucking my face with a vengeance. Every demand I followed. Not executing came with severe punishment, and tonight I wasn't in the mood to scream tears of pleasurable pain while she opened my asshole with her realistic strap. She climaxed with such intensity that caused mountains to move. Relieved. My thoughts. But suddenly she cleared her voice, which meant she wanted me to strap up. She was about to wear me out. As fast as I could, I strapped up. She was on all 4's. Before I could enter, she turned around and wrapped her hands around my neck, squeezed tight and told me...don't play. I gave her every inch of it. "Sit," she demanded. She had this little love for straddling me while sitting in a chair. She called this the "driver's seat." I gripped her waist as she rode me. She forced her right nipple in my mouth and instructed me to nibble, tug, and squeeze. As in one motion, she hopped up, lied on the edge of the bed; legs spread, she pulled me toward her…then inside her. My hips, in motion with her thrust, caused her to moan loudly. She scratched my back intensively, bit my shoulders mercilessly, and spoke in my ear, "good girl". She climaxed again, and again. Somehow, we ended in the shower with me on my knees tongue fucking her asshole as I rubbed her clit. The shower is where it always ended. We got out, exhausted, which was always how she left me. Without drying off, I plopped on the bed. Sore, tired, and bruised. I smiled to myself. Damn this woman has me doing the most. Before I had an opportunity to catch my breath...she straddled my face

"At any moment I'm going to release every drop of me that has ever been contained."

Orgasmic Thunder

I was awakened by the sound of thunder and her head between my thighs. The latter is what sent sparks through my body causing my back to arch immediately. Lightning flashes lit our dark space. During those moments, I caught her starring up at me. Her lioness-like eyes were almond shaped and tantalizing. She knew exactly what to do in order for me to reach the pinnacle of my rapture. She savored me. My nectar engulfed her taste buds. My moans, muffled by the sound of thunder, escaped my lips. As she played with my muliebrity, I began to give in. She knew she had me. She always knew. Steady, is how she remained as she allowed the nerve endings in her lips to speak to my soul…summoning me to release for her. My body rose in temperature. Small beads of sweat formed on my epidermis. My change in breathing caused her to grip my thighs and pull me closer. Damn. Because of her, my body gushed. My body shook. Moans got louder. I squirmed. She knew how to calm me down as she held my swollen clitoris in her soft, warm, mouth. After, She climbed on top of me. Feeling my wetness on her stomach after I climaxed was always so satisfying to her. She kissed me deeply. Hands interlocked with mine. Her lips went to my ear…then whispered, "goodnight baby girl."

"Handle me. Fuck me. Wrap your soft lips around my hard, swollen clit and suck. Hands and arms wrapped around my thick thighs. Pull me closer and devour every bit of my purity. When I cum, hold my pearl in your mouth and allow your warmth to calm me."

Free Reign

She made me feel submissive in ways I never knew possible.
Every time I touched her, no matter where, sent electric
waves throughout her body...turning her on. Her body
would squirm, moans escaped her lips, subtle lip biting. It
wasn't exaggerated, but sexy and consenting. Her body was
like a blank canvas and I was free to create art. I learned her
body by the sound of her moans, yelps, breathing, and
screams. She guided, and I executed. I had free reign to do
what I wanted. Whatever action I'd taken, was a reaction
that drove me absolutely insane. She came for me from
sucking breast, pussy grinding, strapping, oral sex, fingering
and damn near climaxed by the slightest touch. I felt like
Picasso creating a work of art, and in those moments I knew
I was a legend. On the flip side, she fucked me in a way that
was dominant, yet sexy. Naturally, she turned me into her
little bitch simply based off anticipation alone. She knew my
body. She knew what drove me crazy and what turned me
on. She knew by my wetness, breathing, squirming, and
swelling of my clit exactly when I was about to cum. With
big lips and a fat tongue, she'd stick her tongue in and out
my honey well, while telling me how pink and good I tasted.
She'd taste me and moan. She'd taste me and cum. She
tasted me as if my pussy was sacred. She'd play with both
nipples just the way I liked and tasted me at the same time
like an Olympian pro. Never missing a beat. She'd hold my
clit in her mouth after I came cause she knew how sensitive
I was after. She had fat fingers, so she'd finger fuck me while
talking shit when I would scream and run. Seeing me in
pleasurable pain made her even more turned on and
dominant. She wanted me to know my pussy was hers. The
louder I moaned, the more she encouraged me to keep it up.

She'd ride my ass and choke me as she rode me, while asking whom I'd been fucking besides her. She'd open me up and make me take things I never would, like anal sex. Everything was natural...and that made it so sexy. No one was putting on a show. The aggression, the dominance, and submission just flowed. I became addicted.

"Available…neither of us were that, but our desires, in that moment, were as available as they come. We happily engaged in adult fun that was forbidden, yet so easily obtainable. We weren't secrets, just co-workers."

So wrong, So Right

This is so damn wrong but baby you feel so good to me, my thoughts as she scissored me on top of my work desk. We were clit to clit, grinding, both of us masking the cries of pleasures that threatened to escape our lips. She looked down at me, as I looked up at her. Both of us married, yet sexually unfulfilled. Sexual frustrations brought us together last month during a staff meeting. She sat there scrolling through a dating site, unbeknownst that I was eyeballing her phone. I couldn't help but to notice she was scrolling through the women section. I glanced at her wedding ring, then at her. I wondered if she was married to a woman. I was as gay as they came; at least this is what I've always told myself. I too was married. My wife was currently deployed to Afghanistan on a 12-month tour. She was only 3 months in and my libido was through the roof. I knew marrying a soldier was a horrible idea, but it came with its perks. My mind zoned in on the lady sitting in front of me. I leaned toward her and whispered, "Let me know if you find one you like." She looked back at me. Embarrassed. Faked a smile. Locked her phone. Readjusted in her seat. She had no idea that I was her new Regional Manager. Nor did she know that she'd be in my office by the end of business day. This is how it all started. She stood in my office. I told her to come in and have a seat. She sat. I stood and locked the door. She was quiet as I walked back toward her as she sat in her seat. I was close enough to smell the NeiaShea she wore, the best shea butter on the market. This was a familiar scent, which sparked light conversation. I stopped talking and stared into her eyes as she spoke…taking in the beauty of her facial features. I stood, again. Her chair was scooted far enough away from my desk for me to stand in front of her, drop to my knees and spread her thighs. Taken back, she froze; unaware of what was about to take place. I looked at her as my soft hands rubbed smooth thighs. Her eyes gave me consent to continue. Curious fingers brushed against the seat of her blue and purple panties. Feeling the heat radiating from her love nest, I pulled her panties to the side. She grabbed my hands, informed me of her marriage, and yet remained seated. Her words went unheard. Her body told a different narrative in which I chose to attend to. I clenched both thighs and pulled her to the edge of the chair. I was unprepared for her to grab the back of my head to burry my head deep between her thighs. Control, in that moment, shifted. She whined her hips like a Caribbean girl against my agape mouth. The music that flowed from her vocal cords was a harmonic melody of tension and release. As she climaxed, she gripped her fingers around my hair, pulled me in, and kept me steady as she drifted to a mental state of sexual elevation. As we fast forward to today, while she scissors me on top of my work desk, I can't help but to look up at a woman who has been able to sexually fulfill me in ways my wife has never. Total bliss is a necessary state of mind when you are enjoying every second of the extreme climaxes of a love affair.

"We're not supposed to be fucking." Her last words as she creamed all over my chin. *"I know,"* My response, in between licking her dry.

Emotional Lover

Emotional lover. That's me. Vowing to never put myself in a casual situation that would leave me...hurt. Yet, my body and mind rebelled against my better judgment. I became intimate with her that night. I gave into her. With her, I was submerged in intense feeling. Overwhelming, yet inviting. I needed every bit of her as our chest rose and fell in unison. She was my guitar. As I plucked her strings she created melodies and harmonies unheard of. I was addicted to her song. I desired to be the woman who continuously created, within her, freedom of expression. She had me in ways unknown to she, and I. In that moment, of bliss and weakness, I gave myself away to a woman who looked at me as just another fish in a sea of many. Before she got a chance to know me, I had given her me in the most intimate way. Delicate, was my heart. Fragile, was that of my spirit. Empty, how I am left feeling. Something so beautiful and sweet turned sour. Emotional lover. That's me. Vowing to never put myself in a casual situation that would leave me...hurt.

"In the beginning I impressed her. Every bit of my existence was intriguing. To her, I was a breath of fresh air. Oxygen she needed. Her reason to live."

Good Girl

She's pushed me up against the wall and wrapped her hands around my neck. She missed me in ways she could only express physiologically. She kissed me. I matched her yen for me. Nothing is what she wore. My favorite. I smirked. Bit her neck. I slipped 2 fingers insider her, saying hello to her soul. Then 3...then 4. I loved the way her moans became silent. Eyes closed tight, she braced herself. Pussy clinched tight around my fat fingers. With my knees, still standing against the wall, I divided her thighs further. She found her voice again. In between pleasurable pain she begged me to wrap my lips around her clit. My smirk was replaced with a scowl. She knew better. I slipped my fingers out of her pussy faster than she enjoyed. Her neck, I grabbed. Medium pressure. She moaned. Shut the fuck up. She obeyed. I sucked and bit her lips...then her neck. I ordered her to the bed, on her stomach. She lies there, waiting. I slapped her fat ass, again and again. She buried her head in the pillows. I began rubbing her ass, slowing her breathing. Before she could exhale, I slipped 4 fingers inside her womanhood. Then 5. She screeched. Grabbed the sheets. Issuing out pain excited me. The more she screamed, the harder I fucked her. Her body began trembling. Vaginal walls pulsated on wet fingers. She was about to orgasm. I stopped. I grabbed a hand full of her hair and wrapped it around clenched fist. "Did I tell you to cum for me?" She shook her head no, and readjusted between mute moans and deep breaths. I was aroused. She was the reason. Ordering her on her back, I positioned my head in-between thick thighs and devoured her pussy. Her reaction to me gave me all the ammunition needed to keep going. With my lips and tongue, I massaged her in a sacred place. I sensed her climaxing. Allowing her to release in my mouth, I moaned in unison with her. While her body shook violently, I ordered her on top of me. She knew the drill. She stood up on the bed. I lied down on my back. I spread my legs. She scissored me...clit directly on top of mine. She rode me slow. She was still sensitive. I slapped her fat ass demanding that she rode me faster...and harder. Disobeying my orders came with consequences she didn't enjoy. She obliged. It was something about forcing her to orgasm a second time that gave me pleasure. She tried to ease up. I grabbed her waist and sat her back down. Guiding her with my gyrating hips sent chills through her spine. It caused her to grip my thigh, tilt her head back, and squirt all over me. "Good girl." I expressed.

"She's a victim of her own desires."

Phantom

I squeezed my legs tight. Got control of my short, choppy breaths. My eyes were closed. I lie alone but my thoughts...on her. She was a woman I wanted to be an explorer of my body. I needed her tongue to be a voyager of my inner being. I needed her to treat my temple as if it were her world map. Mouth agape...my back arched as phantom fingertips, lips and tongue traveled every inch of my flesh; sucking and licking me in virgin spots. Unintentionally taking my breath away. My thighs parted. My own fingers separated my labia majora. Moans escaped my parted lips as I touched my throbbing clit. Right there. I whispered to a woman who was not present. I imagined her tasting me as if she loved it. Loved me. Shivers...my body in response to that thought. Her thick, fleshy tongue entered my tight hole devouring my wetness. Soft hands massaged my inner thighs. My voice...lost. My body spoke on its behalf. I imagine she trailing her tongue back to my pearl, thick lips taking in all of me. I cum. We cum in sync.

"Lately, my womanhood has been questioning whether you're capable of taming her or not. All the talk has me second guessing your skills, or lack there of. Or maybe, I'm just tired of the let down. Expectations have always been somewhat of a disappointment. My high standards are higher than most have been able to reach. Well, what if I'm just over thinking it all? I need you to prove me wrong and put out the fire that burns from within me."

Fuck Toy

Fuck toy. Her very existence was to allow me to fuck her whenever I needed. She relished the thought of submitting to me. I took great pleasure in taking out all my anger deep within her abyss. She just needed a nut most days. I needed a punching bag. Our dynamic was nothing more...nothing less...than what it was. A game of tug-of-war. Days like these, when I'm angry, she was my go to. Unbeknownst to her, I'd strap up while she slept. Enter her from the back...fuck her brains out. No lube. Her pussy naturally moistened when she realized I was in a mood. Damn. I loved how she stayed ready. Accepting my sexual abuse...mixed with intense pleasure. Positions changed. She's on top. Riding. I pinch her nipples. Suck her nipples. She stares in my eyes. I bite my lips. It's too damn intimate. Positions change... I fuck her from the back. Waist gripped by my hands. I thrust inside of her tight pussy as if I give zero fucks. As she cum, positions change. Her swollen clit is being tugged, teased and sucked hard...by me. She squirms. I grip her thighs tighter. She tries to run. I pull her closer. As I suck, I slip 2 fingers inside. Skilled fingers does the come hither motion. Massaging her G-spot. She screams. She cums again for me. I'm not done, cause shit, I'm still angry. I grab her hair and guide her to all fours and tell her to suck my dick. She does. I smile. She opens wide...I go throat deep. She gags. I shiver. Looking at how sexy she is…I began to fantasize. Positions change. While still on all fours, I enter her glory hole. Lubed up, I push deeper. She likes that shit. She grabs a vibrator and plays with her pussy while my strap is deep in her ass hole. Her body is reacting to the strap and myself. I'm wet. The more I open her up from the back, the greater my relaxation. She screams my name.

Again, she is exploding. I wonder if she's exploding from my strap in her ass, or the vibrator on her clit. Maybe it's the double stimulation. Fuck it. I pull out...let her get her shit together. I shower, get dressed, kiss her forehead, and roll out. I'd choose a fuck toy over the gym any day.

"I was never a nonfactor. In fact, even throughout her marriage, although fairly new...I was the forbidden fruit she always desired. The candy she needed to taste. The unfilled fantasy that lingered at the tip her tongue."

Short and Bittersweet

Damn...my thoughts as I tried to escape my constant thoughts of getting fucked like she loved me. It never happened. The opportunities were there but it never happened. Ugh. But shit...that didn't keep me from craving her in the worst way. I mean, my body reacted to touches and feelings only she could fulfill. At least that's what I had convinced myself. She had this sophisticated sexual appeal that drove me crazy. I wanted her to want me. Just as quickly as it started...so delicately, yet passionately...it ended.

"We went there. Disobeying every boundary that we set for ourselves."

In Control Of It All

She wanted to make me fall in love with her...just like old times. As her tongue trailed the surface of my skin, I wanted so bad to get up and leave. I was mad, but I was stuck for more reasons than one. This one being the sexual trance she had me in. Her tongue stopped at my newly painted toes. She knew what that did to me. She opened her mouth and sucked. Instantly, she had me. I was hers. Giving each toe on each foot attention, she made love to my feet like no other woman had ever done. My weakness. She finished. Her fingers slid inside my panties for confirmation. That was an ego booster for her...how soaked I'd become because of her. She stood up. Undressed. Her body was like a work of art. I stared. Mouth watered. With her eyes, she undressed me. I followed suit. She sat up in bed, pulled me on top of her. I straddled her. Her back against the headboard, we sat intertwined. Breathing in sync. Kissing deeply. She knew I couldn't resist the way we catered to each other's physical needs. She grabbed my hair and pulled my head back...bit my neck and shoulders, softly. I inhaled, and then I exhaled. In one swift move, she had me on my back and she on top of me...her pussy on mine. We scissored. This was her favorite. It was something about being in control of it all. My moans echoed throughout the room. Her moans were adlibs to my song...subtle, yet intense. She gyrated and bounced. Our clits connected each time. I felt her body tensing up. She made this sexy face when she was about to cum. Looking at her reactions had me on the border of insanity. She climaxed, which made me cum. We came together. She sat there until her breathing, our breathing, became normal. She got up, slid on her strap, and demanded that I got on all fours. I obliged. I gasped as

40

she entered me from behind. She always did it nice and slow...at first. Grabbing my waist, she guided me on her thick strap. She made me fuck her back when she felt I was slipping from my knees. My ass bounced against her pelvis. She was so damn deep inside me. It felt so good, but right before I came, she slipped it out. She got on her knees, pulled me to the edge of the bed and sucked my aroused clit until I came in her mouth. I screamed as she slipped her tongue deep inside me. She loved the way my vaginal walls contracted around her tongue. She got up, got into bed with me and cuddled me. In that instant I forgot why I was originally mad in the first place. She then stood, slipped into some cute panties, and went downstairs to bring us back up wine. I watched her ass as she walked away. I told myself that she's not off the hook that easy. My mouth is watering for her taste...not wine.

"She says my words are a poetic form of sex. Capable of arousing her most inner thoughts. Mercilessly bringing her brain waves to ultimate peaks. Heating the very blood that runs through her veins. Sensually sending shock waves from the inside out. She says my words, written or spoken, creates gratification in the most intimate form. She is the reason I write."

Impatient

In that moment, all my inhibitions had vanished. I had completely allowed my inner desires to take control. I wanted her. In spite of us meeting for the first time...she turned me on as if she spoke my sexual language. She looked at me with an intensity that triggered my body readiness. I smiled. Blushed. Masking my elevated libido. Her goodbye kiss caused subtle throbs deep within me. Wandering thoughts leading to tightly squeezed thighs. Biting of my lips. Slow...deep breathing. As I lay in bed reminiscing about this woman I met for the first time...I couldn't help but to crave her...impatiently.

"Between she and I, there was a natural flow of sexual transitions and energy."

Epiphany

I was used to making all the rules when it came to my climax limit, which was a one and done kind of thing. This is until I met her. She needed me to understand that there were new heights my body was able to withstand, but it took a woman of patience to help me explore those new heights. I had never had a woman who took the time out to learn my body. She was attentive in such a selfless way. When we were intimate, she made me feel as though her purpose was for me to reach a place of sexual elation that no woman has ever been able to achieve. She kissed me as though she was attempting to confiscate my soul. With her mouth, she tasted me in places inconceivable. The reach of orgasm wasn't the end of our lovemaking; it marked the beginning of gauging how much of her I could take before I became depleted of the ability to orgasm. The way she made my body feel was ineffable. It was the type of feeling that had me opening my eyes to early morning epiphanies, and closing my eyes to late night revelations.

"Last night, I opened her up and spoke her soul's love language."

Italian Fling

"I could taste you every second of the day and I'd still crave your chocolate," Her words, in-between licking every drop of my wetness. "American woman, you're so sweet." I couldn't understand her Italian but it sounded good as I lied there spread eagled, back arched, mouth agape and body trembling. I gripped my panties that she slipped off of me. Again. I climaxed with a vengeance. Maybe it was the erotic, foreign woman staring up at me from below. Skin dark like mine…hair as coily as mine. We were one in the same…except our spoken language. That didn't keep her from asking me up to her small apartment. We met at a coffee shop. She stared. I ignored her until I couldn't. My smile was all she needed to spark an unsuccessful conversation. That small chat, mixed with jumbled sign language, ended with me being invited to her home…for drinks. Why not? I'm in Italy for one more day. She sat close. I dismissed it due to their culture. Her hands touched my thighs. I welcomed her touch. She rubbed her fingers up and down my spine. I didn't stop her. She kissed me. I allowed her tongue to enter my mouth. She guided me down on her small couch with no effort. I was open to what may come. She lifted my dress. Pulled my silk, pink panties down and spread my legs. "May I?" I shook my head yes. Not knowing what she just asked me for. In that instant, I found her face deep between my legs. Tasting me. My breath was taken away. With my mind all over the place, I decided to settle it on the moment…because damn, the moment felt so good to me. She tasted me with her mouth, while her hands trailed my thighs, stomach, breast, and nipples. It's as if she was implanting an image of me in her head, never to be forgotten. She tasted me so sweetly. So soft. So selfishly.

I...am...cuming...again! My swollen clit, trapped in-between her luscious lips, was held captive. I tried to squirm away...she didn't allow me. "I have you exactly where I want you, American woman." There she goes with that Italian shit. It drove me crazy...not being in the know.

"Between my legs, her favorite place to lie. She teases me with kisses that quickly heats up the blood running through my veins. I bite her lips, suck her tongue, and whisper to her how much I want her. She tells me to repeat myself. I oblige between ear lobe nibbles. Half moaning, have speaking, I tell her that I need her."

Just Say When

I can't promise I'll be gentle baby. Just hold me tight as I slide it in slow. I want you to take deep breaths and relax. If you need to scratch me, scratch. If you feel the need to bite, bite. All I need you to do is allow me to lead. I am your pilot in control of your every move. The thought of you beneath me gets me so excited. As I begin to fill you up, inch by inch, talk to me baby. Let me know how you're feeling. While I lay on top of you, gripping your ass beneath you, leave it all up to me to make that pussy talk for me. As I stroke, I listen. Your every reaction causes me to perform a sexual reaction resulting in a satisfying tug of war of cause and effect. The melting of your body and the visible changes of your breathing confirms my total control. Your nails dig into the outer layer of my skin leaving code that translates into love welts with the visible eye. I suck your tongue as I quicken the speed of my thrust. Hands still gripping your ass as you take every inch of me, we moan in unison. Your hands trail the skin of my back until they reach the round of my ass. As you grip my ass while I stroke deep inside of you, you whisper in my ear how much you've needed me. I interlock our fingers and hold our hands above your head. I began sucking your erect nipples as I continue giving you all of my 8 inches. Your feedback has me about to burst prematurely, so I instruct you to get on your knees, head down in the pillow. As I enter you from the back, I grip my hands around your waist. This was your favorite position, and from your gasp, I could tell this position allowed me to reach a spot deep within your hidden place. As I stroke your pussy from the back, I hold your ass cheeks open to watch my strap go in-and out. The sight of your wetness immediately makes my mouth water as I bite my lip and quicken my pace. The sound of your ass slapping against my pelvis masks the sounds of your moans from the rapture your body is currently receiving. I grip a handful of your hair as I fuck you from the back. Your body buckles. I know you are close to climaxing. I need to be face-to-face, breast-to-breast, and eye-to-eye with you as you bust for me. I pull out, lay you on your back, and reenter you so that we could climax simultaneously. As I stroke, we kiss passionately. Your arms are tightly wrapped around my neck as we reached an orgasm that leaves us both limp.

"Hypothetically, if I were there, I'd massage your body down. Allow the energy flowing from within me to soothe you."

Sacred Instrument

She was a sacred instrument, personified. Every stroke of my strap let out high and low notes, creating our own personal opera. Making love to her was like playing my favorite harp. It sent rhythmic chills throughout my body; a love song played by two forbidden lovers in a world who despised our existence. She was my African xylophone. Each high note ignited musical vibes to flow within our bodies, causing our chest cavities to rise and fall in harmonic synchrony. I opened her up with each thrust of my hips. As she stared me in my eyes with such sensuality, she sang an alluring lullaby of moans and grunts that invited me into the very depth of her womanhood. Our lips connected...I sucked her tongue as though she was the mouthpiece of my saxophone. I was determined to blow her in ways that would put out any fire that had ever been ignited, any desires unfilled.

"It's like a never ending void that never gets filled and leaves you hurt too many times to count, unnecessarily."

It's Been A Pleasure

I'm leaned back as she washes my hair. Her hands run delicately through my scalp. It feels so good to me in ways it shouldn't. My eyes closed. I moan. Embarrassed, I cough to muffle the sound. She continues...this time more passionately. I squirm in my seat. It's like her hands are making love to my scalp. Almost as though she knows I enjoy it...a little too much. She asks me how it feels. I jump because her voice has broken my trance. I reply with a simple, "good." With her nails, she scratches my scalp. Her fingertips and palms massage my scalp. I moan again but this time I don't cough. She continues, causing me to subconsciously bite my lips. Before I realize it, she leans in to kiss my lips. Caught off guard, I jump again. She commands that I relax. She straddles me...hands still massaging the shampoo through my scalp...my head still back. She's grinding. I cannot believe what's happening, but I don't want it to stop. My hands grip her thighs as she multitask. She's now rinsing, and then applies conditioner. Still grinding. My hands still gripped around her waist. My hips are now matching the rhythm of hers. She moans low...whispers in my ear that she wanted me the second I walked through the door of the shop. Her hands still rinsing my hair...her breast against my breast...she bites my neck. I hold in my moans because there are clients in the front of the shop. She's now sucking...and her pace has picked up. I feel her trembling on top of me. The water stops. She has climaxed. In sync, she climaxed and finished washing my hair. She stays seated. I open my eyes to find her glaring into mine. She leans over and grabs a large towel...wraps it around my wet locs which matches the wetness of my pussy.

She gets up. Grabs my hand. Walks me to my loctician. Tells me it's been a pleasure.

"A new desire occupied every thought that crossed her mind. She had been introduced to a new sexual lifestyle that had her curious in the most uninhibited form. Not yet having the pleasure to satisfy the new heightened craving...she obsessed over the moment she'd finally get to act out every scene that had run through her head. Life in her 30s had just begun, and each day her boundaries, limits, and apprehensions were diminishing."

Broken Celibacy

I was 36 months celibate, and 3.6 hours was all it took to break that celibacy. Why? I can't answer, but she woke my insides up in a manner that had never before been experienced. See, men were beginning to irk my nerves causing me to lose all sexual desire for them, period. I had not realized that I was in the middle of a sexual orientation transition, until I met her. She was a Goddess in human form. This woman had me feeling like an adolescent. I was curious in ways that I was unfamiliar with. We met at a 'Paint and Sip' spot. My painting, which was equivalent to that of a kindergartener's, wasn't what one would call a masterpiece. Her painting, on the other hand, was absolutely beautiful. My glare went from her painting to her eyes. Our eyes locked. Not wanting to be caught staring, I told her that she and her painting were stunning. She was quiet for a second. Her eyes trailing my body, she finally spoke, inviting me over to her home to talk about…art. Caught off guard with her request, but being the extroverted risk taker that I am, I took her up on that offer. We gathered our paintings, purses, and headed to our cars. She gave me her address in case I got lost while following her to her home. Her home was as beautiful and well put together as she was. She offered me wine, I accepted. 3 hours later we were on her couch, giggling and talking about everything under the sun from far away galaxies, politics, and unfortunate toxic traits that people embrace. There was a brief silence. I felt soft hands on my thighs. I jumped because, well, I don't know why I jumped. She told me that she wanted me the moment I sat down on the stool to paint. She expressed to me that she had no idea that I was into women, but when I complimented her looks that gave her all the confidence she needed to invite me over for wine and conversation. I corrected her by saying I was not into women. In fact, I told her that I had never been with a woman. She asked me why did I come? I had no answer. She asked me again. I told her because I wanted to. She asked why? I had no answer. She leaned in to kiss me. At first I hesitated to kiss her back, but her smell, softness, and feminine energy drew me in like a love spell. She stood up, took my hand, guided me to her bedroom. She looked me in my eyes and told me that tonight she wanted to be my first experience. I wasn't sure if this was a statement or a question, but my lack of response was all the response she needed to undress me and lie me down on her bed. Delicately, she kissed, licked, and sucked the surface of my skin as though I tasted of honey. My body began reacting in different ways, which frightened me at first. I was in a nervous bliss. Masking my moans was something that was only happening inside my head. Every so often she'd ask me if I was ok. Between deep breathing, and uncontrollable body shivers, I managed to shake my head yes. After making a mental map of all of my erogenous zones, she traced her tongue and lips down to my swollen pearl. I closed my legs because I knew that she already had me on the brink of orgasm without tasting me. Gently, she parted my thighs, looked up at me and told me to just let go. As she wrapped her large, succulent lips around my pearl, I felt a huge gush flow from deep within me. The sounds coming from within me were sounds that have never escaped me before. Oh my goodness was all I could say over and over as I gripped her natural hair to keep her from continuing to suck my pearl. I had never cum so fast. I was a bit embarrassed. She got up, lied beside me, and cuddled me. I felt so safe in her arms. As she fell asleep I couldn't help but wonder why it took me so long to realize that women were the substance I was missing in my life. I listened to her heavy breathing. I listened to her heartbeat. I took in her sweet smell. When she wakes up, I wonder if she would allow me to explore her. I want to make her feel just as good as she has me feeling right now. I closed my eyes and drifted off to dreamland.

"A new feeling immediately took over my body like electricity traveling up wet steel. I was completely shocked. Back arched. Mouth agape. Eyes opened wide. I gasped for air. Like previous toys before this one, I wasn't expecting anything major. But, this one took my breath away like a thief in the night. On the verge of climaxing, I knew that I was hooked."

Sneaky Link

She had to be sneaky when it came to our sexual escapades. Home was not her safe haven. It was rather a place of chaos, nosiness, and the occasional pop up visits of the ex. Something about being caught by her mama or ex wife made my pussy throb. Being with her made me feel like a bad girl; a woman who wasn't supposed to be doing what she was doing, yet, I did. She had this "girl next door" type of look with a body to die for. I knew the moment she messaged me on this dating site that I wanted to engage in sexual escapades with her. The feeling was mutual. What I wasn't expecting was the whole "high school experience" with the sneaking around to avoid being caught. At first it was a turn off. After a while, watching her struggle to control her loud moans became somewhat of a sexual game for me. I wanted to see how far I could go before we got caught, not by her kids, but low-key by her mama. Actually, I wanted her ex to pop up. The thought of her answering the door, red in the face and out of breath gave me a smile of satisfaction. Yes, I knew this right here wasn't anything long-term, but the sex was good and I enjoyed the thrill. She sucked my clit like a cherry blow pop. Tossed my salad like a vegetarian. Strapped me mercilessly beyond satisfactory. Had me feeling like a 30-year-old virgin. This girl introduced me to whips, chains, handcuffs, gag-balls, floggers, rope, hot wax, and paddles to name a few. Just when I thought I had experienced it all, she shows up in my life with a smirk.

"There's something about words, both written and spoken, that exhilarates me in the worst way."

Drunken Request

"You want me to stop," as I pulled her panties to the side with my teeth. Her thighs parted allowing me easier access. She was giving me the silent treatment. However, her body was not. The thought of me fucking her best friend wasn't the problem, it was the way I fucked her. We were poly. Precious encounters were breathtaking, but this time, she rejected the entire experience. Soft moans escaped her lips. Subtle rocking of her pelvis against my thick tongue let me know that I was slowly knocking down that wall of anger that she had instantly built as her best friend creamed all over my chin. Being poly came with rules. Rule number one, no eating another bitch's pussy. Only she had the privilege of feeling rhapsodies that only I had been able to give her. However, during a drunken moment, she had given me permission to orally milk her best friend dry. Without a thought, I dove in headfirst. Shit, best friend was hesitant but willing to experience what my girl bragged about since our partnership. Besties' curiosity was written in the way her pussy instantly dripped sweet morning dew at the thought of hearing my girl telling me to taste her the way I did she. My focus drifted back to the current moment I'm having with my girl. I taste the inside of her walls. Something about the way her walls pulsated against my thick, pink tongue sent chills up my spine. I'm addicted to the pussy. Her pussy. The way her body responds to me is overwhelmingly satisfying. I suck...lick...finger fuck her at the same time. Satisfying her makes me moan. As she watches me sucking her clit, she notices that I am about to climax. Her moaning and breathing quickens. My hips are grinding against the bed as I wrap my arms tightly around her thighs. I need her steady. As I bounce my head on her womanhood, I moan in anticipation of us climaxing in unison. This gets her ass every time. Her clit swells in my mouth. My lady parts are creating a puddle beneath me. We are in a place of no return. She grabs my head, arches her back, and allows herself to release in the warmth of my mouth. Tasting that sweet nectar instantly causes me to latch my lips around her clit while I cum to the sounds and reactions of her. She has caught her breath. I rest my head on her thick thighs. She asks, "So this is how you ate my best friend's pussy?"

"It turns me on to be an element of shock. Little, freaky ways about myself that hides behind a shy smile and smirk. Being underestimated is a bit of a turn on to me. Catching her off guard when she becomes my canvas. Leaving her speechless and bashful. This...is an unintentional skill of mine that I have grown to embrace and look forward to."

Sex Note

Hey ma'. You know I love tasting you. I lick with intention, and I suck with ambition. Damn, I love the way you cum for me. Girl you have me feeling like I'm obsessed with you. You have me so gone in the head now. I love making your toes curl. Open up, I want to feast and feed your soul girl. I love the way you taste when I get you soak and wet. I want you on your back, thighs spread, skin to skin, lying in the bed girl. Making love to the sound of your breathing. Hold me close when you get loud. Ima' make you so damn proud.

Sincerely,

Bae'

"She was the personification of every thought that lingered in the forefront of my mind."

Let Me Show You

"Let me show you how to do it," her words as she guided my head down between her thighs. I was super excited to please a woman who was 10 years my senior. She was 31. Something about an older woman had always turned me on, but I had never thought I'd actually be able to fulfill such a fantasy. When the time came, which is the current situation, I got too excited and she quickly put an end to it. She told me not to feel ashamed, but to take my time with her. As she guided my head down, she instructed me to spread her labia majora, and to suck her clit directly. She enjoyed direct pleasure. She said, "Don't forget to suck and lick at the same time. I want to feel those lips and that tongue baby." I obliged, which caused her body to tense up in satisfaction. She guided my hands to her nipples. "Learning how to multi-task while remaining focused is what I need you to perfect, baby." As I followed her instructions, I made sure to focus on pleasuring her pussy and nipples at the same time, without losing focus. "Don't stop playing with my nipples baby." Shit. I lost focus! Just when I thought I was the shit in the bedroom, an older woman shows up and humbles the shit out of me. "It be like that sometimes," Is what she would say. I continued stimulating her nipples like she liked. I paid attention to her body's reaction, her breathing, and the tensing up of her muscles as she grinded her hips. "That's it baby," she stated in between moans. Yes! Was all I could think. "Don't stop," she expressed as I removed my fingers from her nipples to grip her thighs. Shit! I lost focus just that quick! I continued stimulating her the way she needed me to. "I'm about to cum baby," she exclaimed! Before I knew it, she had squirted in my mouth and all over my chin. I continued sucking and licking, paying

69

attention to her body's reaction. "Slip two fingers inside of me and do the come-hither motion, baby! Hurry!" I did as I was told. She screamed and creamed all over my fingers. She reached down and slowly slid my fingers out of her. "You made this pussy feel so good. Good girl," she spoke as she sucked her nectar from my fingers. I blushed. I was excited to master the art of making her cum in various ways. I needed her to become addicted of this young thing. Hell, I was already addicted to her.

"She was younger. Every move she made was calculated and fresh. She presented a sexual gift I never knew I needed. An enticing high that lies dormant within my sexual compound. With her, I felt alive. Free. No boundaries. No silent judgments…just the ability of an uninhibited mind."

Sexual Submission

She was a lady of little words, but her sex appeal spoke a lot. So much went unsaid vocally, but so much was stated in the way she non-verbally expressed her desires. I had been her little sex slave for 4 years now. Honestly, our dynamic was fulfilling in various ways, but the foundation was sexual. We both wanted it that way. In the beginning, I had to learn her in every way. I had to learn her every desire, every fantasy, every like, love, hate, and turn off. In order to serve her the way I needed and wanted to, I had to study her every chance I got. It was difficult. Her method of training was by paying attention to detail. Not much was said. She hated to repeat herself. Her number one rule was to pay attention and learn her. That was new for me, but I embraced this change and new challenge. It was something about this lady that had me willing to go outside myself. See, outside of her grace, I was a dominant woman in every aspect of my life. In her presence, I was her submissive. My desire and need to serve her sexually was intoxicating. If you know, you know. Over the years, she has opened me up to erogenous zones I never knew existed. She has made me orgasm in ways I never knew were possible. Before her, my sexual experiences were limited to women who were selfish and unaware of how to properly please a woman to fulfillment. My Dom, also known as my Mistress, taught me that sex was a selfless act that should be taken seriously. She taught me sex was a form of art. Because of her, I am now on the path of opening up my own sex therapy practice where I can teach others all I have learned from my dynamic with my Dom. As I mentioned, our dynamic is a beneficial one, I fulfill her every desire when she needs me to. She takes me to new heights both in and outside of the bedroom. Her sexual slave is what I desire to be. It's what I crave. It's what I dream of at night when I am not in her presence.

"A weekend getaway turned into having unexpected sex each evening. Despite my reservations about giving in to her touch, my body betrayed every promise between it and my brain. Funny how things work."

Trust Me

It wasn't about being able to take it all on the first try. Trusting me to open her up little by little until she swallowed me whole was my goal. However long that took, I was patient enough to wait, on her. Anal play wasn't her thing. After many nightly discussions, she surrendered to me in a way she had never done before. For that, I owed her an enjoyable first experience. I was determined to introduce her to a new possible pleasure that maybe, just maybe she'd enjoy. Our weekend adult store run ended with the purchase of some silicone anal satisfier beads. These were the ideal beginner beads she needed for anal training. It was now the moment I had been waiting for, her complete submission to me. She lies there on her stomach as I kissed her round ass all over. I took my time exploring her. I Spread her cheeks and licked the sensitive skin, which surrounded the opening of her anus. Anal play, in any form was foreign to her, but the sound of low moans and the sound of heavy breathing gave me the green light to keep going. Simultaneously, I firmly, yet gently massaged her ass cheeks as I spread them apart to enter her from behind. Slowly, I entered my tongued deep in her ass hole. She gasped, gyrated her hips, and gripped the sheets. I slipped my tongue out and repeated. I asked her if she was ok, and she responded, "Yes baby." I feasted on her until I felt her trembling and heard the escalation in her moans. I expressed to her that I was now about to use the anal beads. I needed her to mentally be aware of every step. I needed her to know that, although she had fully submitted to me by trusting me, she was still heard and respected. She nodded that she was ready. I instructed her to get on all fours, arch her back, and to put her head down on the pillow. As I generously lubricated the beads and her ass, I felt myself trembling from anticipation and the sight of her ass being readily available to me. I began inserting an anal bead. I felt her body tensing as she moaned in slight pain. I stopped applying pressure and said, "Breathe baby. Try to relax your body as much as you can." When she was ready for me to continue, I reapplied pressure to the first anal bead. The tightness of her asshole made my mouth water, again, but I knew I had to remain focused on the task at hand. Listening to her moan, and watching her as she bite her lip while still allowing me to enter her, had me soaked. I finally got the first anal bead in. I began to softly, bite, kiss, and suck her ass cheeks while I allowed to anal bead to stay inside of her. I wanted her body to get used to the feeling. "You did good baby." She smiled and asked me to keep going. I obliged. There were five anal beads, each one bigger than the one before it in order to open her up and get her ready for real intercourse. I was turned on that she was willing to advance to anal bead number 2. I applied more lube then began applying pressure to the second anal bead. She yelped. I eased up and began to walk her through it as I did during the first round. Eventually, the second anal bead entered her asshole. Again, I left it in so that she could get used to the feeling of having something inside of her. "Damn baby, you're doing so good for me," I told her as I leaned forward to deep kiss her. I slowly pulled the beads out of her, laid her on her stomach and hungrily feasted on her pretty little ass. As I feasted she began to let out sounds of pleasure, She trembled vehemently. She screamed out, "Fuck, I'm about to...!" As I continued to feast, I couldn't help but smile to myself. Mission accomplished.

"Just thinking about what you do to me makes my temperature elevate and breathing change."

Femme Fatale

She had never been with a femme. To her, a femme was the type of woman who lied there and followed suit. Never a guide. Never one to take control in any situation outside of her work environment. Then she met me. A femme who possessed everything she desired in a woman. I was a femme who was independent, dominant in more ways than one, and sexually uninhibited with the ability to bring her to a sexual trance that would leave her mentally and physically recovering for days. I told her that making love was my love language…100 steps beyond physical touch. All it took was one night with her to debunk every myth that had ever been created about femmes. I took my time with her, had her trembling just at the thought of what was to come. Doubt was thrown out the back door, when I slowly undressed her while staring her in the eye. As she stood, I kissed her from her neck, to her collarbone, breast, nipples, stomach, stopping at her pelvis. With my soft hands, I guided her legs apart. I parted her vaginal lips with my pink tongue. She gulped, tilted her head back, and closed her eyes. My delicate hands gripped her ass, pulling her closer as I greedily sucked her clitoris. Her hips gyrated against my full lips. My tongued massaged her swollen pearl causing her muscles to convulse. I looked up at her. I was enjoying the way her body was reacting to my physical touch. I rose up and instructed her to get on her knees. She felt my hands caressing her ass. Then soft lips kissed her ass. Then teeth nibbled her ass cheeks. I spread her and slipped my thick, wet tongue in her anus, which caused her to moan with intensity. I slid my tongue out and trailed the groove of her anus. She felt my soft fingers brush across her pussy. I sucked my fingers as I positioned myself on top of her in the 69 position. She opened her mouth as she invited my womanhood in for a taste. As I sucked her clitoris, softly, yet aggressively, she squirmed beneath me. She sucked my clit, matching my rhythm. Then, I started bobbing my head. Her lips loosed around my clit as she tried to muffle her screams of gratification. As she regained her composer, her tongue and lips found my sensitive clit again. The weight of my body on top of her was enough in itself to make her cum, but I was not ready for her to cum yet. Feeling the way my body squirmed, the way I grinded my hips, and the low feminine moans as I sucked, bobbed and licked her clit were breathtaking to her. She said, " I can't believe you feel so good to me." Later she told me I was the definition of one's sexual love language. All of a sudden, she lost her composer and she exploded. Tears ran down her eyes. It's like our spirits locked and wouldn't let go causing our intimate connection to overflow. Unbeknownst to her, I climaxed during her climax. We were now face-to-face, breast-to-breast, her legs spread…me in-between them. Her chest rose and fell. Then, I slide one, then two fingers inside her. My two middle fingers explored her vaginal walls, resting on her g-spot. I began massaging her g-spot, slowly, yet with the right amount of pressure. Her breathing accelerated. I sucked her right nipple as I massaged her insides. Low whispers in her ears encouraged her to release without holding back. She was now in a state of total submission as her body released, squirting all over my pink and white sheets, creating a puddle of her womanhood beneath her. I slid my fingers out of here, laid down in-between her thighs on my stomach, and licked her dry. Each lick was like a screenshot of our sexual encounter. I was the type of femme that ignited a fire within her that only a certain type of fuel would be able to put out.

"You are my morning brew. The coffee that wakes me...the caffeine my brain craves."

Dirty

I like it dirty. I want to taste and smell you in your natural. Your natural musk is an aphrodisiac. This is when you taste the sweetest. Your feminine hygiene is as sweet as honey in its most raw state; a scent untouched. Give me you in the most purest form and allow me to engulf myself in the essence of your aroma…that of unadulterated euphoria. There's something about your savoring redolence that draws me in and takes me to a place of no return. Staring at your honey-well has my mouth watering with relish; anticipating a flow of cream that's always accompanied by descriptive, incomprehensible words of enjoyment. Fighting the impulse to violate your body in the most intimate way has my breathing elevated. Instead, I draw a mental map of your anatomy to store in my hippocampus. Laying out a memory map of your body's subconscious responses as I explore the entirety of your epidermis. Each stroke of my fingertips against your soft skin, deliberate. Each measured brush of breast against breast…intentional. Providing your body with a heightened level of libido, and denying its need to a swift release has the both us in a trancelike state. This moment is teaching me the importance of not reacting to your responses in a hurried manner…a moment that is teaching you to enjoy the journey without anticipating the climax. Each moan is a beautiful invitation to give into you. Just as much as I like it dirty, your weakness was when I did you dirty. Leaning over, I kiss you with a painful passion that has you begging me to finally give you what you have been desiring from the moment I lied you down on silk sheets. Turning you on your stomach, I mount your plump ass. As I grind my pussy on your ass, you grind your ass into my pussy. My breast lay against the bare skin of your back. I reach beneath you and pull your head back as I grip and suck your delicate neck. Just as quickly as I mounted you, I explode. Licking my femininity off your ass, in between love bites and delayed shivers, was a prerequisite to devouring your melting pot. Turning you on your back, I slip two, then three fingers inside of you. The outcome of busting all over your body resulted in complete saturation of your sacred spot. This…was my kryptonite. With three thick fingers inside, I wrapped full lips around your swollen pearl and sucked with a vengeance. Resting comfortably in-between your spread things, gave me the view I need to watch your facial expressions. Scenic views of parted lips with no audible escapes told a story or pure fulfillment with happy endings.

"I can read your words all day. You're intimately poetic in your expression."

Note from the author:

I hope that you enjoyed reading *LITTLE BOOK OF QUICKIES: Unfulfilled Desires*. Although I wrote these micro-reads with the intention of igniting emotion, desires, and juicy conversation, I want you all to continue to practice safe sex. Please know your status and the status of your sexual partner. There's nothing more gratifying than being aware. One more thing, if you enjoyed the book, please don't forget to leave a review. Until next time, may you fulfill your every desire.

-Ro Desire

Printed in Great Britain
by Amazon

67159297R00050